MIKE YOUNG

SUPERTED
KICKS UP THE DUST

Illustrations by
Rob Lee and Bryan Jones

Muller, Blond & White

A tiny aeroplane brushed across the treetops, rustling the leaves and startling the forest birds. It dipped into a clearing and shot straight through the window of SuperTed's treehouse.

Tucked inside the aeroplane was a letter. As the aircraft landed, the letter sailed across the room, straight into the hands of SuperTed's friend, Spottyman. He opened the envelope with a smile.

"Who is it from?" asked SuperTed.

"It's from a museum in the Middle East," replied Spotty. "They want me to take some cosmic dust to exhibit in their treasure room. I must go. It's a great honour."

SuperTed tried to persuade Spotty not to go.

"I think it's a crazy idea," he said. "If you leave the cosmic dust in a museum, someone might steal it."

Spotty would not listen. He thought SuperTed was being very awkward, and he struggled into his rocket pack.

"If Texas Pete gets hold of that cosmic dust, he'll try to bring all the villains in the world back to life!" argued SuperTed, but it was too late. Spotty was already launching himself off the platform and soon he was shooting across the morning sky.

SuperTed thought for a moment. "Spotty is taking a terrible risk," he said. "I think I'd better say my magic word." In a flash, he changed into his special form.

A few moments later, he was following Spotty eastwards across the sky.

Meanwhile, in a city in the Middle East, a small crowd was gathering to watch a very unusual performance. On the steps of the museum was a very strange belly dancer.

The dancer was dressed as a woman, but looked very much like a rather fat man. He seemed to be wearing a wig and was muttering to himself in a deep, masculine voice. It was Bulk in disguise.

While the guards peered in amazement at this extraordinary sight, Texas Pete and Skeleton sneaked up the steps towards the museum. They were not looking for ordinary treasure. They had heard about the cosmic dust.

They entered the building as Bulk finished his routine with a shout of *"olé!"*

Inside, the curator of the museum was showing Spotty around. They were walking through a huge hall, full of statues, paintings and jewels.

"Here you can see the treasures of the greatest empires of the world," explained the curator.

"But is it safe from thieves?" asked Spotty, who was beginning to feel a little uneasy at the sight of so much riches.

"Of course," answered the curator. "We have all sorts of burglar and fire alarms." Then he stepped forward and asked Spotty to place the cosmic dust in a specially prepared showcase.

By now, Bulk had joined Texas Pete and Skeleton and they were all creeping through the corridors of the museum. Skeleton peered into a glass case, full of fabulous jewels.

"Ooh, Tex," he whispered. "Look at that necklace . . . and that bracelet. They're so shiny and glossy and lustrous. Can't we steal them?"

"No," answered Tex. "We came here to get that cosmic dust. When we've stolen that, we'll be able to take anything we want."

Skeleton wanted the jewels so badly that he was not prepared to take "no" for an answer. He turned to Bulk and whispered. "Go on, Bulk. Break the glass."

Of course, only Tex was clever enough to realise that there was a burglar alarm. Before he had time to warn the others, Bulk brought his fist down on the display case. There was a tinkling of glass and then, all over the building, bells started to ring.

In the treasure room, Spotty heard the alarm and began to panic. There were burglars in the museum! He snatched the jar of cosmic dust and began to run.

At that moment, Tex ran into the hall, followed by Bulk and Skeleton. Tex followed Spotty, but Bulk and Skeleton headed for the balcony that ran along the top of the hall. They ran round on both sides of the room and, clinging to some long curtains, began to swing down towards Spotty.

Luckily, Spotty saw what was happening. He ducked out of the way just in time and Bulk and Skeleton hurtled straight into Tex.

As the three villains picked themselves up from the floor, Spotty staggered out of the treasure room into a corridor. The excitement of the chase had left him breathless and he rested for a moment against a statue of a three-headed dog.

As he did so, a small amount of cosmic dust spilled out of the jar he was holding, and drifted up towards the statue. The eyes of the statue opened, and the three faces of the dog began to come to life.

Spotty heard Tex and the others running towards him, so he stumbled onwards into another hall.

Tex and his cronies stopped near the statue and paused. "Where did that pinhead go?" snarled Tex, as they looked up and down. Then each of them let out a fearful yell. The three-headed dog had come to life and bitten them all.

The chase was still not over. Spotty ran on to a parapet that skirted the roof of the museum, but he was not quiet enough. Tex heard his footsteps and was quick to follow.

As they all ran across the roof, a red shape passed overhead. SuperTed had arrived. Without anyone seeing him, he opened a window in the roof and slipped inside.

He was going to teach them all a lesson.

Spotty ran back into the museum. Tex was getting closer and closer. No matter how fast Spotty tried to run, he could not get away and at last Tex leapt forward and grabbed him around the legs.

Of course, Spotty fell flat on his face, and the jar of cosmic dust flew into the air. Skeleton caught it and passed it straight to Bulk.

"Wow, thanks," said Bulk. Nobody had ever trusted him with anything important before. Now, surrounded by Greek statues, he felt like an Olympic runner, carrying the flame to the games. He ran proudly forward, and smashed the jar down in front of a statute of Poseidon, the Greek sea god.

A cloud of cosmic dust rose into the air.

Suddenly, they all gasped with fright as the huge statue started to move towards them.

"Do something, Tex!" screamed Skeleton. But Tex could only stand and gape as the stone figure began to rise into the air.

The three villains turned to run, but the sea god hurled his three-pronged spear after them, pinning them to the ground. Then the statue turned towards Spotty.

"And now for you," it said in a deep voice. "You have angered the sea god. You have meddled with the laws of nature!"

It was interrupted by the sound of a fire alarm. Suddenly, the front of the statue seemed to drop away. "Oh no, the heat from my boots has set off the alarm system!" said a familiar voice.

It was not a statue after all, it was SuperTed.

Later, Spotty claimed that he knew it was SuperTed all the time and that he was not frightened by the statue at all.

SuperTed knew the truth, but what really mattered was that everything had ended happily. The thieves had been caught. SuperTed had rescued what was left of the cosmic dust and they had mixed some fake dust for the curator to exhibit in the museum.

As they said goodbye, there was only one doubt in SuperTed's mind. Somewhere in the museum, there might still be a statue that had been brought to life with cosmic dust.

Books in the SuperTed series